For Emily Mullen,

a very special girl

First published in Great Britain in 2013 by Simon and Schuster UK Ltd
A CBS COMPANY

Text copyright © Michelle Misra and Linda Chapman, 2013
Illustrations copyright © Samantha Chaffey, 2013
Designed by Amy Cooper

The right of Michelle Misra, Linda Chapman and Samantha Chaffey to be identified
as the authors and illustrator of this work has been asserted by them in accordance with
sections 77 and 78 of the Copyright, Designs and Patents Act, 1988.

1 3 5 7 9 10 8 6 4 2

Simon & Schuster UK Ltd
1st Floor, 222 Gray's Inn Road
London
WC1X 8HB

Simon & Schuster Australia, Sydney

Simon & Schuster India, New Delhi

A CIP catalogue record for this book is available from the British Library.

PB ISBN: 978-0-85707-623-6
eBook ISBN: 978-1-47111-724-4

Printed and bound by CPI Group (UK) Ltd, Croydon, CR0 4YY
www.simonandschuster.co.uk
www.simonandschuster.com.au

www.michellemisra.com

New Friends

MICHELLE MISRA

SIMON & SCHUSTER

Poppy

Ella

Tilly

Archangel
Grace

Jess

Primrose

1
A New School

'Oh, wow!' Ella Brown breathed as she looked through the big golden gates. On the other side of them was a castle made of pure glass. It sparkled like a diamond in the sunshine. Ella's wings fluttered. The Guardian Angel Academy.

It was just how she had always imagined it would be – totally perfect!

Ella checked her reflection in the shining gates. Her white halo was sitting straight, her brown, shoulder-length hair was glossy, and her green eyes sparkled. She couldn't wait to start her very first day!

She reached for the bell but, before she could press it, the gates swung open. A long driveway led to the castle entrance, parting fields of wild flowers. Bright butterflies flew from flower to flower and the gentle sound of bees hummed in the air.

Angel-tastic! This was going to be such fun! Ella half skipped and half flew forward, her tiny wings fluttering as they carried her along the drive. There were bound to be lots of adventures in store at angel school. She flew up and pirouetted at the thought.

'OK, so how *do* you do that?'

Ella spun round to see a very tall girl, about her own age, behind her. The girl was dressed in the same pearly-white uniform as Ella but she didn't look like your average neat and tidy angel. Her dress already had dirty splodges on it and a tangle of blonde curls were scrambling out from under her halo.

'Do what?' Ella asked, surprised.

'Make your wings work like that!' The girl peered over her shoulder at her own wings. 'I've been trying to make mine work ever since they appeared, but they just don't seem to. Look!' She jumped up in the air. Her wings gave a few faint flaps but didn't manage to lift her up. 'Oh, I'm useless!'

'No you're not. It just takes practice,'

Ella told her. I just think fluttery thoughts. Imagine you're a butterfly, swooping and gliding . . .' Ella was picturing it so clearly that her own wings fluttered and she rose into the air. 'Like that!'

she giggled, floating down again.

The tall girl concentrated hard. 'OK, here goes. I'm imagining, I'm imagining . . .'

'Keep on trying. You can do it!' Ella encouraged. The other girl's wings started to flutter faster and suddenly she shot up into the sky like a rocket.

'Whoa!' she cried in alarm, turning a loop-the-loop and coming down again, her arms flailing. She would have crashed to the ground but Ella rushed forward to catch her just in time.

'Thank you!' gasped the other girl. A grin lit up her face. 'Hey, I flew! I really flew! I might not have won any marks for style, but I did it – and it felt totally brilliant.' She hugged Ella, almost knocking her over. 'So what's your name? I'm Poppy.'

'I'm Ella,' Ella replied.

'And is it your first day too?' Poppy asked.

Ella nodded.

'Can we be friends?' Poppy said, giving her a hopeful look.

'Well . . .' Ella paused teasingly. 'Do you like adventures?'

'Oh yes!' breathed Poppy.

Ella broke into a smile. 'Then we can be *best* friends!'

Poppy grinned. 'That's totally *cherub-azing!*'

Ella linked arms with her and looked up at the glittering castle. 'Look out, Guardian Angel Academy. Here we come!'

2
Crash Landing!

Ella and Poppy hurried down the driveway. On one side there was a mysterious wood of tall green trees. 'You know, we could always go and have a little explore,' Ella said.

'OK,' Poppy said, eagerly. They set off towards the trees.

'Where are you two going?' a shrill voice exclaimed from behind them.

They swung round. Another angel about their age was flying down the driveway. She looked absolutely perfect, her golden hair was curled into ringlets and her white uniform was spotless. 'Were you about to go in the woods?'

'Possibly,' Ella replied cautiously.

The blonde angel folded her arms. 'The school rules say we should go straight to school. Don't you know angels should never break rules?' She stuck her nose in the air. 'Mummy was right. She said that I would probably meet some badly brought-up angels when I got here.'

'That's a horrible thing to say!' Poppy protested.

The blonde angel looked her up and down. 'Halos and wings, look at you! Have you been dragged through a hedge on your way here? Haven't you read the school handbook?' She pulled a book out from the pocket in her uniform and smugly read out. 'For your information: *Angels should strive to be neat and tidy at all times.* That's what it says here on page one. Along with: *Angels should always obey school rules.*' She gave Ella a pointed look and, tossing her ringlets back, she flew on her way.

'I think *she* must have missed the page that says angels should be kind and polite at all times.' Ella exclaimed.

Poppy giggled. 'I suppose she is right, though, and we probably shouldn't break the rules on our very first day!'

They headed after the snooty angel. Getting closer to the castle, they saw that there were angels everywhere. Most of them were older than Ella and Poppy and were flying effortlessly.

'Isn't the castle massive?' sighed Poppy, looking up at the glittering turrets. Craning her head, she tripped over a stone and promptly fell over.

'Oh my goodness, are you all right?' An older angel flew over as Ella helped Poppy up. 'I'm guessing you must be Poppy and Ella,' she said. 'I've been looking out for you. My name is Seraphina. I'm a Guardian Angel and a teacher here.'

'I like your halo.' Ella gazed at Seraphina's glittering diamond halo.

'Thank you.' Seraphina looked pleased. 'It hasn't always been so special. When you start at the Academy you have a white halo but they change as you prove what a good angel you are.'

Ella knew that. White became sapphire, sapphire became ruby, ruby became emerald and so on, until eventually gold became diamond. It was the same with the uniform – that changed colour too, and your wings grew bigger and more downy and feathery with each change in halo colour. If you had a diamond halo by the end of your seven years at the Academy you would become a Guardian Angel when you graduated, and then you could be a teacher or go to the human world and protect people.

'I finished at the Academy last term,' said Seraphina, her wings glowing as they changed with every colour of the rainbow. 'And now I'm going to be the form tutor for the new first years, so you'll be seeing quite a lot of me! Now, come with me and I'll show you round.'

She led them through the big front door.

Ella and Poppy both gasped as they looked round the huge hall. White fluffy clouds bobbed about and, through them, they could see a ceiling covered with iridescent moons and stars. It was set against a dark background, making it look like the most magical starry night ever. Chandeliers hung down and a spiral staircase led upwards in the centre of the room.

'It's brilliant,' whispered Poppy.

'Totally glittery!' said Ella.

'It is rather amazing, isn't it?' Seraphina agreed. Another angel with a diamond halo passed by with three young angels following her. She smiled at the girls and said hello to Seraphina before guiding her girls up the staircase. 'That's Angel Celestine, she teaches Angel Gardening,' said Seraphina.

'You both have beautiful names,' Poppy said.

'They're your angel names, aren't they?' said Ella.

Seraphina nodded. 'I can see you've been reading your handbook, Ella. Excellent!'

Ella blushed. Despite what the angel on the drive had said, she did in fact know the handbook off by heart. It had all the basic angel rules in it. When angels finished at the Academy and became a Guardian Angel, they were also given a special angel name. She wondered what hers would be – if she ever got to be a Guardian Angel that is!

'Now let me show you to your dorm.' Seraphina led them up the spiral staircase. On the first floor there was a circular hall where assemblies were held and the dining hall where they would eat their meals. On the second floor there was a maze of different classrooms. On the third floor there were six corridors leading away from the spiral staircase into different turrets. 'The first year dorms are down there.' Seraphina pointed to a nearby corridor with planets all over the walls and ceiling. 'We could fly to your dorm if you like.'

'Great!' exclaimed Ella.

'Er, OK,' Poppy said doubtfully.

Ella screwed her face up in concentration. Her wings started to beat and she flew into the corridor.

'Not too fast now, Ella!' called Seraphina.

But Ella just couldn't help herself. She wanted to impress Seraphina and she was enjoying the feeling of the wind rushing past her. Flying was easy! She went faster and faster, thinking how angel-tastic she must look. Yippee!

'Ella! Please slow down!' Seraphina cried anxiously.

'I'm fine!' Ella called. 'I really am!' But just then, the door of one the dorms opened and two angels came out. There was nothing Ella could do.

'Whoa!' she yelled as she collided with them.

Crash!

All three angels landed in a tangled heap on the floor!

3
Magical Dorms

'I'm sorry!' Ella gasped. One of the angels had red, shoulder-length hair and a disdainful expression. The other angel was blonde. 'Not you again!' she snapped at Ella.

Ella groaned inwardly. Oh no. Of all the angels in the school she'd gone and crashed into the angel they had met earlier.

Ella hastily held out her hand. 'I really am sorry. Here, let me help you up.'

The blonde angel ignored her hand and snorted. 'I'd far rather you helped me by staying out of my way! *Completely* out of it!' She scrambled to her feet. Her halo was now sitting crookedly on her head and there was a smudge of dirt on her face.

Seraphina landed beside them.

'Come along now, Primrose. I know you're upset, but Ella *has* just apologised to you.'

All traces of anger vanished from Primrose's face as she saw the teacher. 'I'm sorry, Angel Seraphina,' she said, blinking contritely. 'It was just such an awful shock and I was ever so worried in case my new friend, Veronica, had been hurt in any way.' She looked at the redheaded angel with a sweet and caring expression.

Seraphina nodded kindly. 'I understand, my

dear. Now back into your dorm please.'

Primrose and Veronica went back into their dorm. Seraphina turned and looked at Ella. Ella bit her lip, expecting to see anger in the teacher's eyes, but there was only a look of sadness. Somehow that made her feel even worse.

'Ella, why did you ignore me?' Seraphina said softly. 'I asked you to slow down.'

'I know. I'm sorry.' Ella hung her head. 'I was just so excited with it being the first day and, well, I suppose I was showing off a bit,' she admitted. 'It was really stupid of me, Angel Seraphina. I am really very sorry.' She swallowed.

There was a pause. 'That is very honest of you,' Seraphina said. 'And honesty is a good quality for an angel to have. You know, I think we shall say no more about it. However, in future, you really must do as you're told or you'll never become a Guardian Angel.

Now –' Seraphina's tone changed '– why don't you and Poppy come and meet your dorm-mates?' Ella looked up and saw two other angels looking out of a door at the end of the corridor. One had light brown hair and a dreamy expression, and the other was small with a long, dark ponytail and looked sporty. She and Poppy followed Seraphina over.

'This is Tilly,' Seraphina said, nodding at the girl with the light brown hair.

'And I'm Jessica, but call me Jess,' said the smaller girl, smiling.

'I'll leave you four to get to know each other,' said Seraphina. 'See you at supper time.' And with that, she flew away.

'Well, that certainly was some arrival!' said Tilly, grinning at Ella.

'Crashing into Primrose of all people too,' said Jess, her brown eyes wide.

'Forget about it now,' Tilly told Ella. 'Come into our dorm!'

Going inside, Ella gasped. There was a large oval window looking out over the grounds as well as four white wardrobes and four dressing-tables, each with one of their names in large golden letters. A statue of a golden dove on a perch swung from the ceiling high above their heads. But it wasn't those things that made Ella gasp most. She was staring at the beds. They looked like floating clouds, but with duvets and pillows on them! One was rose-pink, one lilac, one aquamarine and one pale green.

'Cupid's arrow!' said Ella, as the clouds jostled around the room.

'They're the comfiest things ever,' said Tilly, scrambling on to the aquamarine cloud. 'The lilac is yours, Ella, and the pink one is Poppy's.'

Ella and Poppy ran to their clouds. Poppy hesitated for a moment.

'Don't worry,' Jess said, seeing her face. 'I was worried too at first, but tell yourself you won't fall through and you won't. Just jump on!'

Ella jumped on. She squealed as she sank into it. It was the softest, most wonderful bed ever!

'You can make them move around by flapping your wings,' said Tilly. 'We can play tag!'

Soon all four of them were zipping about, giggling as they chased each other. Ella thought it was fantastic! They finally stopped, panting and happy.

'Our dorm is definitely the best!' declared Ella in delight.

'The very best!' the other three grinned.

4
Exciting News

After about fifteen minutes, the golden dove opened its mouth and started to coo.

'That means it's supper time!' said Jess. 'It's cloudberry leaves and golden pie tonight!'

'Yum! My favourite!' said Ella.

'We always have starflower salad for supper on Mondays at home,' said Tilly, rather sadly.

'I don't care what we have for supper, just so long as we eat!' said Poppy. 'I'm starving. Come on!'

They all ran downstairs. There were angels everywhere! The youngest angels were easily spotted because of their white dresses and halos, and smaller wings.

There were four long tables in the dining hall for the students, each loaded up with silver platters of the most delicious-looking food, and another table for the teachers. A plump angel with very wise eyes, enormous gossamer wings and dark hair coiled in a bun was sitting at the head of the table.

'That's Archangel Grace,' whispered Jess.

Ella looked over in awe at the headteacher of the Guardian Angel Academy. Archangels were the most important angels you could get. She'd heard so many amazing stories of the good deeds Archangel Grace had performed as a Guardian Angel in the human world. It must be incredible to be a Guardian Angel and have lots of adventures.

'I wonder where we should sit . . .' Tilly said.

Poppy headed for a table, but Ella grabbed her arm. 'Not there!' Further along the table, Primrose

and Veronica were sitting down. Primrose's hands were crossed neatly on the table, her face looking angelic. But as she caught sight of Ella and Poppy, she scowled.

Quickly, Ella turned away. Finding seats on a different table, they sat down.

There was a loud peal of bells and everyone tucked in.

Ella had never had such a feast. Just when she thought she couldn't manage another thing,

towers of rainbow jelly appeared on each table with massive bowls of the creamiest ice cream!

She was just finishing her bowl when Archangel Grace stood up.

'Greetings, my angels,' she announced in a silvery voice. 'Once again it is the start of a new term here at the Guardian Angel Academy. Please will you all welcome the new first years.' Everyone round the room burst into applause. Archangel Grace eventually held up her hand for silence.

'And at the end of this week there will be a special start-of-term garden party for all angels who have earned at least one halo stamp.'

'Hooray!' the angels cheered.

'What are halo stamps?' Poppy whispered to the others.

Ella knew, but didn't want to speak while Archangel Grace was talking. Luckily the headteacher went on to explain. 'For the benefit of our new students who may not have read the handbook completely, all students have a halo card.' As she spoke, golden nightingales fluttered in and dropped a card in front of each of the new students.

Ella picked hers up. It seemed to be just a normal piece of card.

'Every time you do something good – either in work or for behaviour – you get a stamp on your

halo card,' Archangel Grace explained. 'When the card is completely filled, your halo will change colour and your wings grow a little bigger. Be warned though,' – Archangel Grace's face became serious – 'halo stamps can also be removed for breaking the rules or not behaving in an angelic way. But now let us turn our minds to happier things. Enjoy this evening, angels, and tomorrow your first lessons will begin!'

She sat down and everyone started to talk. 'I wonder what our first lesson will be?' said Poppy.

'It's flying!' said Ella, who'd read the timetable in the handbook.

'Brilliant!' exclaimed Tilly. 'We're going to have to get really good at that if we're going to become Guardian Angels one day!'

There was a snort behind her. Ella turned. Primrose and Veronica were standing there.

'Guardian Angels!' Primrose said scornfully. 'You lot are never going to make Guardian Angels! You might as well just leave now!'

Sticking her nose in the air, Primrose linked arms with Veronica and flew away.

Ella opened her mouth, but just in time saw Seraphina watching them and bit back her sharp retort. She really mustn't get into trouble again. 'Primrose is so annoying!' she hissed to her friends.

'Forget about her. Think of nice things,' Jess advised. 'Like our flying lesson tomorrow.'

'And the start-of-term garden party!' put in Poppy.

'*If* we all have a halo stamp,' Tilly added anxiously. 'What if we don't?'

Ella quickly forgot Primrose. 'We will!' she declared. 'We'll all be at that party and we're all going to have some fun this week, just wait and see!'

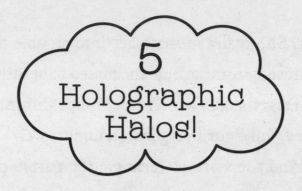

5
Holographic Halos!

When Ella woke the next morning, for a moment she couldn't remember where she was. But then, when she saw the golden light streaming through the window and felt the comfy cloud beneath her, she knew *exactly* where she was. The Guardian Angel Academy!

'Whoa!' she grinned, as her cloud started shifting beneath her. She quickly flapped her wings until her cloud moved downwards and her feet touched the ground.

'Good night?' Jess asked, as she stretched and yawned, her eyes cloudy with sleep.

'The best!' grinned Ella.

'I was dreaming about home,' said Tilly. For a moment she looked sad. 'It's lovely here, but I do miss my family,' she sighed.

'There's no time for missing anyone now,' Poppy said cheerfully, pointing at the golden dove as it let out a morning greeting. 'It's time we got up and got dressed or we'll be late for breakfast!'

The four girls scrambled out of bed.

☆ ☆ ☆

It was very busy in the dining hall. There was everything you could possibly want for breakfast – sparkly muffins, towers of toast, the creamiest porridge, and juices in every colour of the rainbow. Once Ella had finished, she picked up her bowl and beaker and went over to where an older angel with ruby-coloured wings was carefully stacking a trolley and muttering under her breath.

'Nearly dropped it . . . not another,' she groaned.

'Let me help you with that,' offered Ella.

'Oh you *are* an angel!' The older angel smiled, laughing at her own joke. 'Thanks. My name's Holly by the way.'

'And I'm Ella,' said Ella.

Ella and Holly worked happily alongside each other, with one collecting and the other stacking. As Ella piled up another bowl, a voice came from

behind her.

'It's not every day a new angel helps out without even being asked.'

Ella spun round. 'Archangel Grace!'

'I think you've earned yourself a halo stamp!' Archangel Grace beamed. 'Come to my office to collect it.'

A halo stamp? Ella couldn't believe her luck. 'Thank you,' she said excitedly as the headteacher disappeared. She couldn't wait to get it and tell the others!

'Go on,' said Holly, seeming to read her mind. 'Go and get your stamp, I can finish up here.'

'Sure?' asked Ella.

'Positive,' said Holly.

Quickly, Ella made her way out of the dining hall and up to the corridor where the Archangel's office was. She stopped outside, nervously fingering her halo card. One . . . two . . . three.

Ella knocked on the door.

'Come in!' called Archangel Grace.

Ella was lost for words as she looked around the Archangel's office. It was just amazing! Little golden bells of all shapes and sizes were hanging from the ceiling and, as a breeze fluttered through an open window, they chimed musically. Archangel Grace smiled from behind her glass desk, a large book spread out before her, little half-moon glasses perched on the end of her nose.

'What's that?' Ella asked curiously, pointing at the book.

'This?' Archangel Grace smiled. 'It's a map book of the whole of Angel World, my dear. Take a look, if you like.'

Ella stepped forward to look at the beautiful pages. Even upside down, she could see bubbling brooks and fields of poppies. As Archangel Grace turned the page, the hum of bees and butterflies sounded around the room.

'It makes a noise.' Ella jumped back, surprised.

Archangel Grace chuckled to herself. 'That, my dear, is the beauty of angel magic. Now, your halo stamp. Have you got your card?'

Ella nodded and held it out.

She watched closely as Archangel Grace took out a little pot of glittery powder from her pocket.

'Angel dust,' Archangel Grace explained, sprinkling a pinch over Ella's card.

Poof! The most beautiful holographic stamp appeared on the card; it shone like silver. Ella felt a warm glow flood through her and felt as if her own real halo was glittering more brightly too.

'Wow!' she breathed.

'Your first halo stamp is very precious,'

Archangel Grace said seriously. 'I can still remember mine. Now, off you go – you've got flying class, haven't you?'

'I have. And thank you again, Archangel Grace,' breathed Ella.

As Ella closed the door behind her, she looked again at the little stamp shimmering and sparkling on the card. It was just perfect! She felt she could have stood looking at it all day, but just then the bell rang. Ella jumped. Quick! It was time for flying class and she didn't want to be late . . .

6
High in the Sky!

'Now angels, remember you don't need to move too much to raise yourselves off the ground. Just fill your head with floaty thoughts. Gently, gently...' Raffaella, the flying teacher, called out. 'And remember, don't go too high or too near the trees!'

Ella closed her eyes and tried to remember

everything she'd been taught. 'Breathe and imagine,' she muttered under her breath, filling her head with thoughts of butterflies and bees. To her delight, her feet began to lift off the ground. She was flying!

'How are you doing, Ella?' Poppy giggled, her arms flailing as she came over. 'I'm doing loads better than yesterday. Whoa!' she cried, as she lost control and spun round. In a moment, the two girls had crashed, before collapsing in a heap on the ground. But Ella didn't mind and in no time at all they were back in the air again.

'That's it, girls, keep up the good work,' Raffaella encouraged. 'You'll soon be flying well. Now remember please, no flying out of the school grounds while you're first years.'

'Not at all, Angel Raffaella? But I wanted to go to Rainbow's End,' said Primrose, swooping over.

'I'm afraid that is completely out of bounds, Primrose.' Raffaella looked serious.

'In that case of course I won't go there,' said Primrose meekly.

'What's Rainbow's End?' Ella asked her friends.

'It's a really magical place,' Tilly explained. 'You can only reach it by using a rainbow near the school. It's meant to be the most beautiful place ever.'

'That's right, Ella,' Raffaella said, overhearing. 'Not only is Rainbow's End a very beautiful place, but a very special flower grows there – the remembering flower. It's purple and, when someone touches it, it makes them feel happy.'

'How does it do that?' asked Ella.

'Ah, that is the subject of another lesson,' said Raffaella with a smile. 'You'll find out all about the remembering flower when you learn about magical plants. But this is a flying class. It's flying time, angels!'

Once Raffaella had moved on to help some of the others, Poppy flew back to Ella and nudged her. 'So did you get your stamp?'

Ella had been longing to let the others see her card with its stamp, but hadn't wanted to show off. 'Yes,' she admitted.

Primrose was still hovering near them. She snorted. 'The Archangel must be mad to give you a halo stamp, Ella Brown!'

Ella ignored her.

'Let's see it then,' said Tilly.

Ella held out her halo card.

'Wow!' Poppy breathed as she stared at the beautiful stamp. 'Our dorm's first halo stamp!'

Ella grinned. 'We'll all have one soon,

I bet we will.'

'As if!' Primrose said. Suddenly she dived forwards, grabbed Ella's card and flew off!

'Hey!' Ella cried indignantly. 'Come back!'

Primrose hovered in the air. 'If you want it – come and get it!' She flew higher.

'Don't, Ella,' said Jess. 'She'll soon get bored and come down.'

But Ella flung herself into the air.

'Ella!' Poppy exclaimed. 'Don't!'

Ella didn't listen. She chased after Primrose. They went higher and higher towards the treetops. It took a few moments before Raffaella noticed what they were doing.

'Come back here, you two!' she cried, but both Ella and Primrose were too far away to hear her. Primrose was flying as fast as she could, but Ella was gaining on her. Whizzing forward,

Ella grabbed at her card.

'*Arrgh!*' Primrose called as, caught off-balance, she fell into one of the trees. Her gown and wings caught on the branches there and, for a moment, she dangled from it like a piece of washing. She shrieked and struggled.

Ella looked at her in alarm. 'Stay still! I'll help you.'

'Get away from me!' Primrose screamed at her as the angels below all noticed and started to laugh and point.

Raffaella was already racing up to the trees. Within seconds she had reached the two girls and was untangling Primrose from the branches. Then she brought them back down to land.

'What in heaven did you think you were doing?' she exclaimed. 'Didn't you hear me tell you not to fly too close to the trees? Look at you – your

white dresses have got dirt all over them and the arms of them are ripped.'

Primrose let out a loud wail as she looked down at her ruined clothes. 'This is all your fault,' she said accusingly to Ella.

'My fault!' Ella was indignant. 'You're the one who took my card and—'

'Enough!' Raffaella held up her hand. 'This is *both* of your faults. And so I'm *de*-awarding you one halo stamp each.'

'*De*-awarding?' For a moment Ella couldn't think what Raffaella meant, but after a second it started to sink in. She was taking a halo stamp away! Ella gaped. That was so unfair! She couldn't lose her precious halo stamp.

Primrose hung her head. 'I haven't got a halo stamp to lose yet, Angel Raffaella.'

'Then you'll have to give up the next one you

get,' said Raffaella crossly. 'Now give me your card please, Ella.'

Ella reluctantly did as she was told.

Raffaella touched her wand to Ella's card. There was a flash and then once more the card was just a dull white-grey colour.

'My halo has faded as well,' gasped Ella, looking around her and realising she didn't have quite the same glittery glow surrounding her as she had done since she got the stamp.

'It has indeed,' Raffaella said. 'Now, back to school. You will both go to the Sad Cloud tomorrow as a punishment. I'm very disappointed.'

As she turned to go, Ella turned to her friends. She was trying not to cry.

'Oh, Ella,' said Jess, giving her a hug. 'You must have known Primrose was trying to get you to do something bad so your stamp would be taken away.'

Ella swallowed. 'I know. I just lost my temper. Oh, I'm a useless angel!'

'No you're not. You'll get another stamp in no time at all,' Tilly told her.

A dreadful thought struck Ella. 'But what if I don't? What if that was my one chance this week and now I've messed up?' She looked at her friends in horror. 'What if I don't get to go to the start-of-term garden party after all?'

7
A Special Idea

The next day, Ella had to spend the whole of the morning between breakfast and break in the Sad Cloud with Primrose. The Sad Cloud was a dark cloud floating above the hall with a round room inside it. Everything was dull and grey and there was nothing to do when you were in there but read old books on angel history and the angel rules.

Ella had spent the whole time ignoring Primrose and reading a book called *Famous Angels Past and Present,* while Primrose had spent her time reading out the angel rules from the handbook and smirking. Ella had got back to the dorm just before the others, who had all been at a forgetting spell class.

Jess and Poppy came to find her. 'Hi,' Jess said giving her a sympathetic look. 'Was the Sad Cloud horrible?'

'*Really* horrible,' sighed Ella. 'Just imagine being cooped up with Primrose for all that time!'

The other two shuddered at the thought.

'So how was the class?' Ella went on.

'Great,' said Poppy. 'We were learning how to help people to forget sadness.'

'We got to use our wands and angel magic,' said Jess. 'But because we're such young angels the spells wear off pretty quickly – although Poppy was really good at them.'

'You too. We got a halo stamp each,' Poppy said. She went red. 'Oh! We weren't going to tell you that yet.'

'Don't be silly!' Ella pushed down the stab of jealousy and jumped up and hugged her friends. 'I'm really pleased for you.'

'Really?' said Jess. 'We thought you would mind.'

'Of course not.' The last thing Ella wanted was her friends to feel bad about getting halo stamps. 'I really *am* pleased. Did Tilly get one too?'

'Well, Tilly wasn't there,' said Jess.

'We thought she must be sick and be up here,' said Poppy. 'She was really quiet at breakfast.'

Ella nodded. She'd noticed that Tilly had been very subdued too. 'I wonder where she can be.

Should we go and look for her?'

Poppy looked torn. 'We've got to go and get our stamps. We were told to go to see the Archangel at break time.'

'But then we really should look for Tilly,' said Jess anxiously.

'Look, you go and get your stamps, I'll go and look for Tilly,' said Ella.

And, jumping down off her cloud, she headed off down the corridor.

☆ ☆ ☆

But Tilly wasn't in any of the other dorms. So Ella went down the spiral staircase to the floor below. Some super-keen angels were doing their homework in the classrooms, but there was no sign of Tilly. Where was she? Now she thought about it, Ella realised Tilly had been quiet the evening before too.

She checked the halls and then went outside, walking around the outside of the building, calling Tilly's name. She had almost given up hope of finding her when she suddenly caught sight of her in the school vegetable patch with a rake in her hand.

'Tilly!' Ella said in relief. 'What are you doing out here? Everyone's been worried about you . . .' She broke off as she realised that Tilly had been crying. 'What's the matter?' she asked.

Tilly sniffed, wiping a muddy hand across her face. 'I'm not feeling great.'

'But if you're sick you should be inside. You'll get into trouble and—'

'I'm not sick and it's OK, Seraphina knows I'm here. She said I could come out.' Tilly swallowed. 'I've been feeling really homesick, Ella. I miss my

mum and my dad, and my brothers and sisters too. I couldn't sleep much last night and so I went to see Seraphina after breakfast. She told me I could miss the forgetting class and come out here instead. It reminds me of home, you see. I used to help Mum with the garden.'

Ella put an arm round her. 'You poor thing.

But you'll see your family in the holidays.' She wished there was something she could do. Tilly looked so sad. 'Cheer up. Just think about all the fun things we're learning – and there's the garden party on Saturday to look forward to as well, that's only three days away. We should be concentrating on getting halo stamps so we can go to that! Poppy and Jess both got halo stamps in forgetting class today.'

Tilly looked rather sheepish. 'Actually, I got one this morning too. For helping Seraphina weed the garden.'

'Oh Tilly!' Ella gave her friend a big hug. 'That's great.' Inside she could feel a fluttering of panic. *All* her friends had halo stamps now. That meant they could go to the party. Surely, surely she wasn't going to be the only one left behind. She didn't think she could bear it if that happened!

'Thanks for coming to find me,' said Tilly. 'I'll just go and put this rake away and then I'll come back inside.'

'OK,' said Ella. 'Don't be long. We'll have forgotten what you look like!'

'I won't.' Tilly forced a smile.

☆ ☆ ☆

Ella headed back into the building to tell Poppy and Jess that she had found Tilly. She wished she could think of something to cheer Tilly up. But what?

Ella thought about it. Tilly loved gardening. And what did gardens have in them – not just vegetables, but flowers. Flowers. That was it! And not just any old flower! An idea started to form in Ella's mind. What was it that Raffaella had said earlier about the remembering flower – about how it made people feel happy? Raffaella hadn't said how it worked, but it sounded amazing.

I could get one for Tilly, Ella thought. But then she paused. The flower was at Rainbow's End, and that was out of bounds. It would stop her going to the party altogether if she was caught. But it would be such an adventure and it would help Tilly . . .

Ella felt a leap of excitement. She'd do it! She just needed to get into Archangel's Grace's office and copy the route down. She could go tomorrow morning when everyone went to assembly.

Ella gave a little skip. She was going to have an adventure. She couldn't wait!

8
Rainbow's End

For the rest of that day, Ella tried to make sure Tilly was never alone so she didn't feel homesick. When Seraphina announced there was going to be a quiz competition after supper, Tilly excused herself to go up to the dorm and Ella went with her.

'You don't have to come,' said Tilly.

'I want to,' said Ella. 'What shall we do?'

They settled on drawing. Ella loved drawing and Tilly had a book from home with pictures of the most magical places from around Angel World. She liked tracing the pictures and then colouring them in.

'That's really good,' said Tilly, as Ella finished a drawing of the Angel Academy. She inspected it. 'Glittery! Look, there's Seraphina and Archangel Grace, and you've even drawn the butterflies and dragonflies outside. I wish I could draw like you.'

'It's a pity drawing isn't a proper angel talent,' said Ella.

'I've read somewhere that drawing *is* an important angel skill,' said Tilly.

'It can't be,' Ella pointed out. 'If it was that important we'd have drawing classes and we don't.'

'I guess,' Tilly agreed. 'I do like your picture though.'

Ella smiled. 'Here. You can have it.' She handed it over.

'Thank you!' Tilly tacked it up to the wall by her bed. 'I love it!'

Ella was glad that she had made Tilly happy.

She'll be even happier soon, she thought. Hugging her secret close, Ella smiled to herself as she thought about her plan.

☆ ☆ ☆

The next morning when the bell rang for assembly, Ella hung back. 'You go ahead. I'll be down in a minute,' she told her friends.

Instead of heading for the hall, Ella headed for Archangel Grace's office. She lingered beside a large marble statue of another famous archangel in the corridor, pretending to examine it with great interest, while she waited for the corridor to clear of people. Once she was alone, she hurried to the door. Thinking she heard footsteps behind her she glanced around, but the corridor was empty. It must have been just her imagination.

Heart pounding, Ella knocked on the door.

When there was no answer, she turned the handle. The room was empty and the book was on the desk. Ella shut the door behind her and ran over. She started flicking through the pages, trying to stifle the different sounds that came out as she looked through it. Finally she found it – Rainbow's End. And here – she traced a line with her fingers – was the Guardian Angel Academy. She frowned, looking from one place to the other. It didn't look so far.

Quickly she pulled a little notebook out of her pocket and started to sketch – north to Bluebell Woods via Honeysuckle Way, then West to Craggy Peaks. That bit looked quite complicated, but from there she should be able to see the rainbow. Once she reached it all she had to do was land on it, slide down it and that was that!

Quickly Ella gave it a last once-over – just to check she had it right. Then, stealthily, she put the

pad back in her pocket and crept over to the door. Left . . . Right . . . The coast was clear.

She smiled. "Rainbow's End here I come," she said.

Behind the statue, an angel with big blue eyes hid and watched her . . .

☆ ☆ ☆

Ella couldn't wait to get going, but one look at the weather outside, as she made her way down to the assembly hall, told her that she would have to wait. The rain was lashing down hard and the clouds were dark and gloomy.

The next day was just the same. And the one after. It wasn't until Saturday that the weather improved. As Ella pushed back the curtains and sunlight flooded the dorm, excitement flooded through her. Today was the day!

The only blot on her happiness was the thought of the party later on. She still hadn't managed to get another halo stamp and if she didn't get one she wouldn't be going to the party. *I'll have to try to do lots of good things when I get back,* she thought.

Hanging behind the others as they headed for their sewing silver linings class, she slipped into the gardens. This was it! Her adventure was about to begin!

In no time at all, she was off. She flew into the air and rose high above the woods, and then swooped across to Honeysuckle Way, breathing in the sweet scent from below. After Honeysuckle Way, it was on to the mountains. It was harder then, the wind blew her this way and that and her route twisted and turned. 'Come on! Keep going!' she muttered to herself. She beat her wings as fast as she could until finally she saw what she was looking for – a perfect rainbow stretched across the sky!

With a final burst of speed, she flew straight to the top of its arch. As she reached it, she was enveloped in a glow of magical colours. She spun round and round for a few seconds before managing to sit down. 'Wow!' she gasped as she started to slide downwards. She went faster and faster, her hair streaming out behind her. A few seconds later, she burst out in a shower of multicoloured sparkles at the end.

She gasped as she bumped on to the soft grass.

Rainbow's End! She was here! Jumping to her feet, she saw that it really was the most magical place. Dragonflies flew from flower to flower and fireflies buzzed in the air. Ella looked all around her at the haze of purple flowers carpeting the grass. There were remembering flowers everywhere! She bent down to pick one up and held it in her hands. She waited for a moment to see if she felt suddenly happy. When she didn't, she turned it round in her hands, lifting up the petals and touching the centre. A riot of sparkles exploded, cascading up around her like a firework display.

'Oh, halos and wings!' Ella breathed. 'Tilly will love it!'

There wasn't time to hang around. Turning from the sparkles, she got out the map. Now to check her way home.

The flower in one hand, map in the other,

Ella spread it out. She was very glad she had it. The journey had been so twisty and turny, getting home without it would be impossible. All the mountains looked the same. But as she pushed it down, the paper flew up as a gust of wind blew across the clearing.

'Oh just stay still for one minute, will you?' she said in exasperation.

Then, just as she was trying to look at the paper, there was an extra-heavy gust of wind and it blew out of her hand! Ella went to catch it but, just as she did, another gust flew it even further away. Every time she neared it, it blew on until, with one last gust of wind, it flew right over the edge of the ravine.

'No!' Ella gasped, but it was no use. The map was gone – and without it she would never find her way back to school!

9
Missing!

'W'here can she have got to?' Poppy said to Jess and Tilly after their sewing silver linings class.

'I don't know,' said Jess, 'but I hope she turns up soon.'

'Looking for your friend by any chance?' a voice asked behind them.

Tilly sighed. 'Come to stir up trouble, Primrose?'

'Trouble? Me?' Primrose looked all innocence. 'Of course not. I just thought maybe you'd like to know where Ella is.'

'Do you know where she is?' Poppy demanded.

'Oh yes. She's gone to Rainbow's End!'

The other three angels stared at her.

'Don't be stupid!' Tilly said. 'Ella's not gone to Rainbow's End. It's out of bounds.'

Primrose tossed her head. 'Well, all I can say is I saw her coming out of Archangel Grace's office three days ago talking about Rainbow's End and holding something that looked like a map. Now she's gone missing. Who's the stupid one now?' She smiled primly. 'Archangel Grace had really better be told about it. After all, first-year angels must never go out of bounds.'

She tossed her ringlets and walked away.

Tilly looked at the others in dismay. 'If Primrose is telling the truth, Ella's going to be in real trouble!'

'Ella wouldn't go to Rainbow's End!' Jess said.

Poppy groaned. 'Well, she does like adventure – she tried to get me to go exploring with her on our very first day, but Primrose stopped us . . .'

'Well this time we've got to stop Primrose telling the Archangel!' Tilly said.

Poppy gasped. 'I know how! . . . Primrose!' she shouted.

Primrose turned. 'Yes?'

Pulling out her wand, Poppy ran towards her. 'Higgle piggle, place a bet, make this angel truly forget.'

'What the—' Primrose's mouth opened and shut as a sparkle of glitter cascaded over her.

She blinked a few times. 'Where am I?' she said
dazedly.

'At angel school,' said Poppy.

'Oh.' Primrose gave her a curious look. 'Who
are you? Are you my friend?'

'Well . . . um . . .'

Primrose looked Poppy up and down. 'You're

not very tidy are you? But I suppose if we're friends, we're friends!' She linked arms with Poppy. 'Hello, friend.'

Poppy sent a help-what-do-I-do-now? look at Jess and Tilly.

'Are you my friends too?' Primrose asked them happily.

'Yes . . . um, I suppose we're your friends,' said Tilly, coming forward.

'You know, I'm sure I was about to go and do something, but I can't seem to remember what it was,' said Primrose, frowning.

'It can't have been anything very important,' Jess said quickly.

'Definitely not,' agreed Poppy and Tilly.

'You're probably right,' agreed Primrose.

Just then, Seraphina walked round the corner. 'Girls, what are you doing here? You're going to be late for your Gardening class.'

'Who are you?' Primrose asked.

Seraphina frowned. 'What do you mean, Primrose?'

'Primrose? Who's Primrose?' said Primrose, looking startled.

'You are, of course,' said Seraphina.

'I'm not Primrose,' said Primrose.

'Is this some sort of a joke?' said Seraphina.

'A joke,' said Primrose indignantly. 'No.'

'We'll just be getting along to class,' Poppy said, hastily.

And with Seraphina watching them in astonishment, the three friends grabbed Primrose and hurried her away.

10
To the Rescue!

Thankfully the next class was Angel Gardening and it was reasonably easy to hide at the bottom of the garden with Primrose, keeping out of the teacher's way. Primrose seemed happy to believe she was their friend, although Veronica kept giving her astounded looks from the other side of the flower beds.

'We're going to have to do something,' Tilly whispered urgently to Jess and Poppy, while Primrose was busy learning how to use magic to persuade sunflower seeds to grow into flowers. 'We might have stopped Primrose telling Archangel Grace for the moment, but the magic will wear off soon and Ella's still missing. We're just lucky that the teachers haven't noticed yet, but it won't be long...'

Jess looked worried. 'Surely she shouldn't be gone this amount of time, even if she has gone to Rainbow's End.'

'Unless...' Tilly swallowed. 'Unless something has happened and she's in trouble?'

Jess bit her lip. 'What are we going to do?'

'There's only one thing for it,' said Poppy. 'We'll have to go after her.'

'But we don't know the way and we haven't

got a map,' Jess pointed out.

'I suppose we could always sneak into Archangel Grace's study,' said Poppy, uncertainly.

They all looked at each other. Even though they wanted to find Ella, none of them liked the idea at all.

'I know!' gasped Tilly suddenly. 'My book! The one I brought from home. It's got pictures of all the most magical places in Angel World. It has a map at the front showing where they all are. It's bound to show where Rainbow's End is!'

'Brilliant!' said Poppy. 'That's a plan then! As soon as gardening is finished let's go!'

☆ ☆ ☆

At the end of the lesson, the three friends took Primrose into the library and sat her down with a thick book called *A History of the Guardian Angel*

Academy. Poppy told her she had to read it all for homework.

'It should keep her busy for a while anyway,' said Poppy as they hurried into the garden. 'Now have you got your book, Tilly?'

Tilly nodded. She'd whizzed back to the dorm while the other two had been in the library. 'Here!' She showed them both the map. 'It looks like we've got to fly over the woods and get to Honeysuckle Way first of all, then head to Craggy Peaks. Come on!'

The three angels stood, side by side and concentrated. Tilly was the first to rise off the ground, then Jess, and finally Poppy shot up like a rocket.

Taking it in turns to read the map and call out directions, they flew over the woods and headed north to Honeysuckle Way before twisting and

turning over the peaks of the mountains. At last the rainbow came in sight.

'Now what?' gasped Jess.

'We fly into it!' said Tilly.

They grabbed each other's hands and plunged into the top. A second later, they were all whizzing down, squealing in delight.

Bump ... bump ... bump ... One by one they landed at Rainbow's End in a flurry of wings.

'Poppy, Jess, Tilly!' Jumping to their feet, they saw Ella standing, staring at them in astonishment. 'What are you three doing here?'

'What do you mean, what are we doing here?' said Poppy. 'We're here because of you, of course! Primrose told us where you had gone.'

'When you didn't come back, we thought you must be in trouble,' said Tilly. 'So we came after you.' She looked round. 'Oh, how glittery! Isn't this an amazing place?'

'Yes, it is, but hang on.' Ella was reeling from what Poppy had said. 'Did you just say Primrose knows I came here?'

'Yes, she saw you coming out of Archangel Grace's office,' said Jess. 'We have to get back!'

'Oh no!' Ella groaned. Her relief at seeing

the others was drowned by dismay. Primrose was bound to tell the teachers. She was going to be in so much trouble. *And not just me*, she thought, looking at her friends. *All of us!*

'Are you OK?' said Poppy. 'Why didn't you come back to school?'

'I lost my map,' Ella said. 'It flew away and I couldn't work out how to get home.'

'Don't worry,' said Poppy. 'We've got a map with us. But we must get back as quickly as possible.'

'Poppy put a forgetting spell on Primrose,' explained Tilly. 'It was so funny, Ella. When Seraphina came along, Primrose couldn't even remember her own name!'

Ella giggled, the seriousness of the situation forgotten for a minute. 'Really? Oh I wish I'd seen that!'

'We left her in the library, but the spell might wear off at any time,' Poppy said. She grabbed Ella's hand. 'Let's go!'

Using the map, they managed to get safely home. One by one, they landed in the gardens, Poppy hitting the ground with a resounding *thud!*

They ran to the library. But Primrose had disappeared!

'Oh no! What if her memory's come back?' said Tilly in alarm.

Ella felt sick. If Primrose had gone to tell Archangel Grace they would all be in so much trouble. Maybe they would even be expelled!

They hurried back to their dorm. Just as they went inside, there was a commotion from further along the corridor. 'Get off me!'

It was Primrose's high-pitched voice. They poked their heads out.

Primrose was being helped back to her own dorm by two older angels.

'It's all right. You'll feel better after a little rest,' one of them was saying soothingly.

'I don't need a rest! I have to keep doing my homework. I have to read the *whole* book!'

'No you don't,' said the older angel. 'You've had a funny turn.'

'Don't be ridiculous,' said Primrose indignantly. 'I'm not feeling funny at all. I'm absolutely fine!'

'Absolutely fine?' The other angel shook her head. 'You couldn't even remember your own name.'

'Of course I know my own name,' said Primrose. 'I'm . . . I'm . . .' She stopped and her voice took on a different tone as she started to frown. 'I am Primrose de-broe Ferguson of

Watersplash Lane!'

'The spell's wearing off!' Poppy hissed.

'Get your hands off me immediately,' Primrose said imperiously. 'I need to see Archangel Grace!'

Jess caught her breath as Primrose pulled free. 'Now what?'

'We've got to stop her!' said Tilly.

'No, wait!' Ella grabbed their arms. 'Let her go to Archangel Grace.' She grinned at their astonished faces. 'I think this could be fun!'

☆ ☆ ☆

Five minutes later and Primrose was outside their door with Archangel Grace. Her voice was full of self-importance.

'Yes, Archangel Grace. I know it's a dreadful thing for an angel to do but, like I said, Ella has gone out of bounds. She's flown to Rainbow's End.'

They could almost hear Primrose shaking her head. 'I simply don't understand how she could behave so badly. Of course, I myself would *never* go out of the school grounds. But then Ella never behaves as a proper angel should.'

There was the low murmur of the Archangel's voice and then the door was pushed open.

'See, Archangel,' Primrose said, 'she's not here . . . Oh!'

Jess, Poppy, Tilly and Ella were sitting on their beds, like perfect picture book angels, polishing their halos.

'But . . . but . . .' Primrose spluttered.

'Hello, Archangel Grace. Hello Primrose,' said Ella innocently. 'Can we help you? We were just taking some time to polish our halos.'

'And very beautiful they are looking too,' Archangel Grace said, before turning and sighing.

'Primrose, I really do not appreciate having my time wasted.'

'But you can't be here!' Primrose spluttered to Ella. 'She went to Rainbow's End!' Primrose turned to the Archangel. 'She *did*!'

Archangel Grace shook her head sadly. 'You're clearly not feeling very well, Primrose dear. I think you'd better spend the rest of the day quietly in bed.'

'But it's the party!' gasped Primrose. 'And I've got a halo stamp.'

'I really don't think it would be wise for you to attend. Come on now, dear. Back to bed. I'll ask one of the older angels to bring you up a tea tray later.'

Primrose took one last look at Ella, Poppy, Jess and Tilly – who were giving her sympathetic looks. '*Gahhhh!*' she cried and she flounced out of the door.

Archangel Grace sighed and shook her head.

'Poor Primrose. She seems very out of sorts today. I'm sorry to have disturbed you, girls.'

She turned to go, when something caught her eye.

'What a beautiful picture.' She pointed to the painting on the wall next to Tilly's bed. She turned to Tilly. 'Is it yours?'

'It is now,' said Tilly. 'But I didn't draw it. Ella did.'

'It's beautiful,' said Archangel Grace. 'Such a good likeness of the school.' She smiled. 'And there I am too. It would look wonderful on my study wall.'

'You can have it!' Tilly said, quickly. She turned to Ella. 'See, I told you so. Drawing *is* a skill.'

'A very highly valued angel skill indeed,' said Archangel Grace. 'Why? Did you think it wasn't, Ella?'

'Well, yes,' Ella admitted. 'We don't have drawing classes, do we? They're not mentioned in the handbook.'

'That's because your handbook is for first-year angels in their first term. You will certainly be doing drawing classes next term and I am sure Angel Gabriella, our Art teacher, will be delighted to know she has such a talented student to teach. Well done on such a lovely picture, Ella. You really must have a halo stamp for it. Come to my study and collect it.'

And with that, she turned on her heel and closed the door. The four friends looked at each other for a moment and then collapsed into giggles.

'See!' said Tilly. 'Didn't I tell you drawing was a talent?'

'And I thought I'd only got a talent for getting into trouble!' Ella said.

Poppy hugged her. 'Now you've got your halo stamp, you can come to the party!'

'While poor Primrose has to stay in bed with a tea tray,' said Tilly. They all giggled again.

'I'm just glad we got back from Rainbow's End without being discovered!' said Jess in relief.

'Why *did* you go there, Ella?' said Tilly.

Ella remembered and, reaching into her pocket, she pulled out the purple flower. It was rather crumpled, but still in one piece. 'I went to get this for Tilly. It's a remembering flower. Do you remember Raffaella told us that they can make people happy? I hoped that if Tilly held it, it might make her less homesick.' She held it out.

Tilly caught her breath. 'Oh, Ella. That's so lovely of you.'

'Try it,' Ella urged. 'You have to touch the centre.'

Tilly took the flower and touched the centre. A fountain of silver sparkles cascaded out, just like they had done back at Rainbow's End. 'It's totally glittery, isn't it?' said Ella happily, as the sparkles filled the air and her three friends squealed. 'I mean anyone's going to feel happier if they're surrounded by sparkles, aren't they?'

'Wait!' said Jess suddenly. 'I don't think it's just the sparkles that make the person holding the flower happier. Look!'

Ella stared. In the centre of the sparkles a picture was forming. It showed four angels, a man, a woman and two little girls.

'Oh my goodness! It's Mum and Dad and my sisters!' cried Tilly. 'Oh wow!' Her face split into a grin as she looked at them.

'It didn't work like that for me,' said Ella, puzzled.

'The flower must work for people who really need it – by showing you people who make you happy!' realised Jess.

'It's wonderful!' said Tilly. 'I love it!'

As she spoke the picture changed and became a picture of Ella, Poppy and Jess all laughing, just as they had been a few moments ago.

'Now it's showing you us!' said Ella in surprise. 'That's odd.'

Tilly's eyes shone. 'No it's not. It's because you all make me happy too!'

Ella, Poppy and Jess all hugged her. After a few moments the sparkles faded. Tilly sighed happily. 'Thank you for my flower, Ella.'

'Do you feel a bit less homesick now?' Ella asked hopefully.

Tilly nodded. 'I really do. Today's been such fun.' She smiled round at them all. 'You know, I think I'm actually just as happy at school as I am at home.'

'Good. Angel school is brilliant!' said Ella.

'And do you know something else that's going to be brilliant?' said Poppy.

They all grinned. 'The party!' they chorused.

The party *was* brilliant. It was held in Archangel Grace's special private garden. Giant butterflies the size of dinner plates fluttered in the air and bright flowers filled the marble pots and tubs. Seraphina was conjuring up sticks of pink cloud candyfloss and Angel Celestine was making lollipops grow on the golden trees. Some of the teachers were playing music so people could dance and, at the end of the garden, there was a massive rainbow slide. It wasn't quite as amazing as sliding down the real rainbow, but it was loads of fun!

'*Whee!*' cried Ella as she whizzed down it.

'*Whee!*' yelled Poppy crashing into her.

They pulled each other to their feet, laughing, and looked to where Jess and Tilly were swinging each other around to the music. 'Hasn't today been great?' said Ella happily.

'Oh yes!' said Poppy. 'Our first real adventure. I hope we have lots more!'

'We will,' Ella promised. 'We really will!' Her eyes sparkled as she looked round the garden. She had a feeling that the fun had only just begun!

JOIN ELLA AND HER FRIENDS FOR
ANOTHER ANGELIC ADVENTURE
IN THE SECOND BOOK IN
THIS SWEET SERIES,

Birthday Surprise

1
An Important Announcement!

'What's going on?' Ella Brown fluttered down the spiral staircase at the Guardian Angel Academy, coming to land at the bottom next to her friend, Tilly. The hallway was crammed full of angels gathered around a notice board, and excited chatter filled the air. *Something* was definitely happening!

'Come and look at this!' Tilly pulled Ella through the crowd. 'Excuse me! Excuse me, please,' she said to the other angels until they reached the front.

The notice was glittery and sparkly and kept

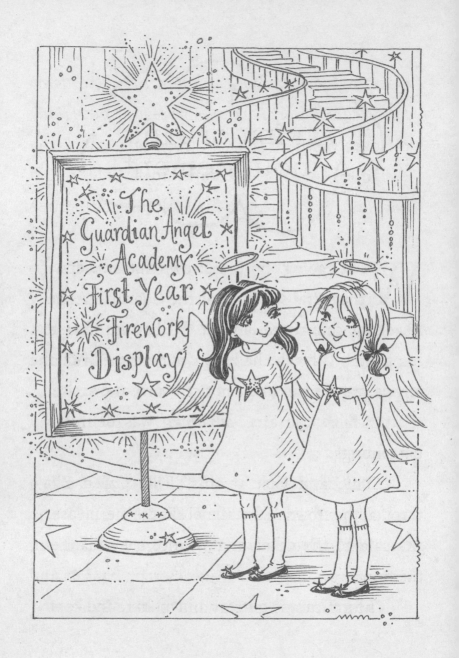

changing colour. *'The Guardian Angel Academy First-Year Firework Display,'* Ella read aloud. *'Friday the twenty-fifth of October.* Oh, angel-tastic!' she exclaimed, pushing her dark brown hair behind her ears. 'We're having a fireworks display in three days' time.'

'I know!' said Tilly, her eyes shining. 'It's the day our parents come to collect us for half term.'

Ella clutched her arm. 'Look – the paper's changing again!' They watched excitedly as the paper turned purple.

Tilly read the words. *'All first-year angels will be expected to take part in the display.'*

Ella caught her breath. 'So we're all going to actually *perform* in the fireworks display?'

'Yes, indeed,' came a voice from behind them. Everyone swung round. Angel Seraphina, Ella and Tilly's form tutor, was standing behind them.

'Every first-year angel will get a turn at carrying the different lights through the sky, and the very best angel will get a starring role in the finale.'

'Oh halos and wings!' breathed Ella.

'That would be really scary,' said Tilly, her eyes wide.

'It would be amazing!' said Ella, imagining everyone watching her as she swooped and dived, setting off fireworks in the sky.

'One thing's for sure, you're all going to have fun whether you have a starring role or not.' Angel Seraphina smiled. 'And I'm sure your parents will enjoy watching the display, before taking you off home for the half-term holiday. However, if you want that starring role you'd better practise your flying.' Angel Seraphina flew away.

Ella turned to Tilly. 'I've seen a fireworks

display before, but to actually take part in one – maybe have the main part – wouldn't that be *totally glittery*!"

'I wouldn't get too excited, Ella Brown,' came a haughty voice from behind them. 'It's not likely *you'll* get the starring role, is it?'

Ella turned and saw Primrose standing behind them. She was the most annoying angel in the whole school. With her sparkling blue eyes, and pretty blonde hair curled into ringlets, she looked perfectly angelic – but she so wasn't.

Ella felt Tilly shrink back – Tilly hated rows – but *she* wasn't scared of Primrose. 'And why shouldn't I get the starring role?' she demanded.

'Didn't you hear what Angel Seraphina said?' Primrose nudged the angel standing beside her, who had red hair and who giggled when prompted. 'Only the *best* angel will get the starring role. And one thing's for certain – you *definitely* don't fall into that category.' Her eyes swept snootily over Ella. 'All you're best at is getting into trouble!'

Ella put her hands on her hips. 'You've been sent to the Sad Cloud as often as me, Primrose.'

'Ella, don't get into a row now,' Tilly pleaded, tugging her arm. 'You heard what Angel Seraphina said – everyone will get to take part in the display. It doesn't really matter who has the starring role.'

'Come on, Veronica.' Primrose turned to her friend. 'We've got better things to do with our time than stand around talking to trouble-makers like Ella.' And with that she flounced off.

'Right! That's it!' Ella sprang after her.

Tilly grabbed her. 'No, Ella! Ignore her. She's just trying to make you mad so you get into trouble.'

Ella slowly brought her temper back under control. Tilly was right. Primrose loved to make her lose her temper – usually when there was a teacher around. Angels were *never* supposed to lose their temper. It said so in the handbook that all the first-year angels had been given a copy of. 'All right, I won't go after her, but she is just so annoying! I hope she doesn't get the starring role in this display.' *And I hope I do,* she added to herself.

'Forget Primrose,' said Tilly. "Let's find the others and tell them all about the fireworks display.'